Granddad's fishing Buddy

Mary Quigley

illustrated by
Stéphane Jorisch

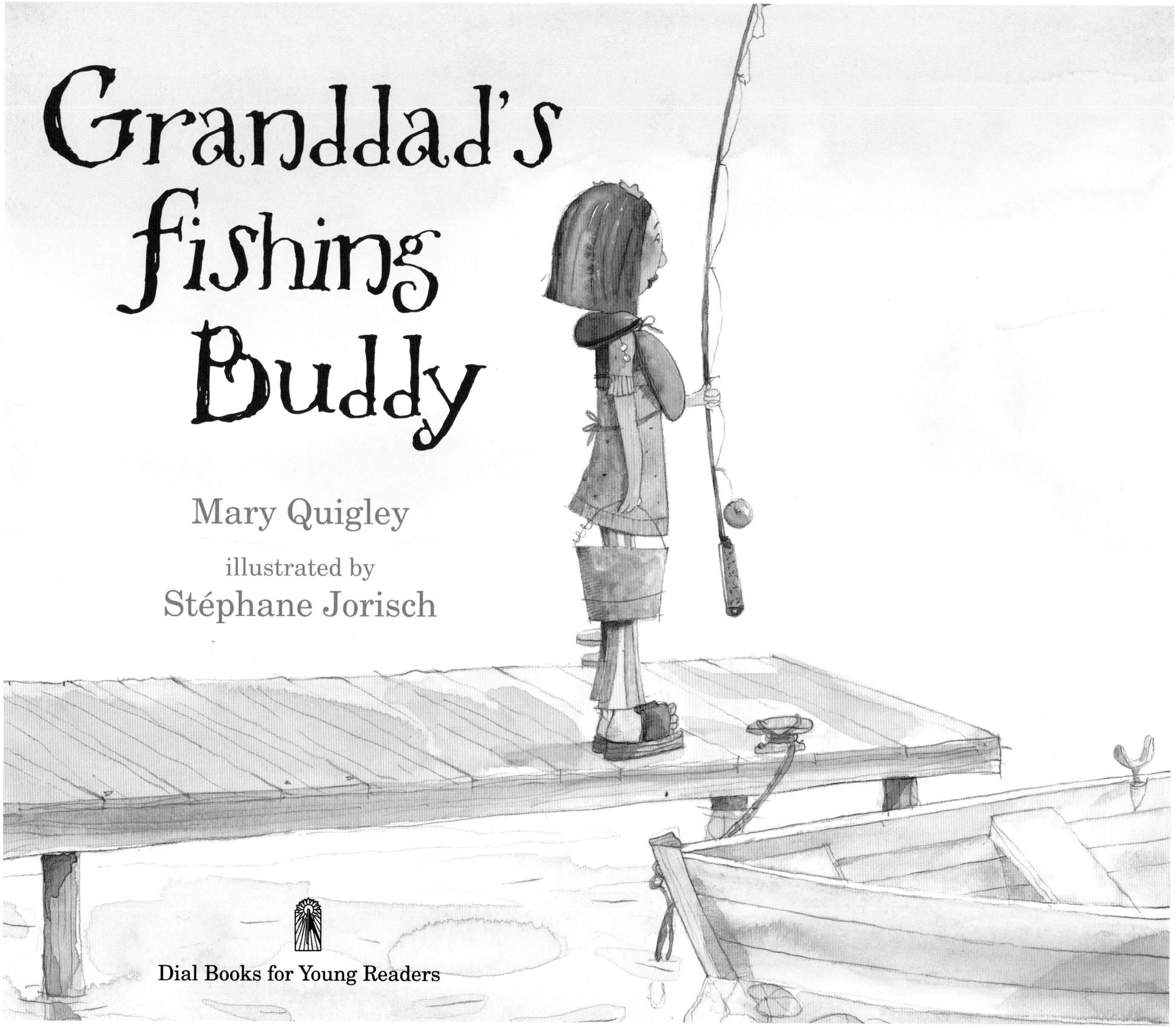

Dial Books for Young Readers

To Dan, for inspiration. To Katie, Colleen, and Megan, for joy. And to the real Grandad.—M.Q.

To the magic of being on water in anything that floats—S.J.

DIAL BOOKS FOR YOUNG READERS • A division of Penguin Young Readers Group • Published by The Penguin Group • Penguin Group (USA) Inc., 375 Hudson Street, New York, NY 10014, U.S.A. • Penguin Group (Canada), 90 Eglinton Avenue East, Suite 700, Toronto, Ontario, Canada M4P 2Y3 (a division of Pearson Penguin Canada Inc.) • Penguin Books Ltd, 80 Strand, London WC2R 0RL, England • Penguin Ireland, 25 St. Stephen's Green, Dublin 2, Ireland (a division of Penguin Books Ltd) • Penguin Group (Australia), 250 Camberwell Road, Camberwell, Victoria 3124, Australia (a division of Pearson Australia Group Pty Ltd) • Penguin Books India Pvt Ltd, 11 Community Centre, Panchsheel Park, New Delhi - 110 017, India • Penguin Group (NZ), Cnr Airborne and Rosedale Roads, Albany, Auckland 1310, New Zealand (a division of Pearson New Zealand Ltd) • Penguin Books (South Africa) (Pty) Ltd, 24 Sturdee Avenue, Rosebank, Johannesburg 2196, South Africa • Penguin Books Ltd, Registered Offices: 80 Strand, London WC2R 0RL, England • Text copyright © 2007 by Mary Quigley • Illustrations copyright © 2007 by Stéphane Jorisch • All rights reserved • The publisher does not have any control over and does not assume any responsibility for author or third-party websites or their content. • Designed by Teresa Kietlinski Dikun • Text set in New Century Schoolbook • Manufactured in China on acid-free paper
10 9 8 7 6 5 4 3 2 1
LIBRARY OF CONGRESS CATALOGING-IN-PUBLICATION DATA • Quigley, Mary, date. • Granddad's fishing buddy / Mary Quigley ; illustrated by Stéphane Jorisch. •   p. cm.
Summary: A young girl and her grandfather go fishing and meet up with the heron that always helps him find fish. • ISBN 978-0-8037-2942-1 • [1. Fishing—Fiction. 2. Grandfathers—Fiction. 3. Herons—Fiction.] I. Jorisch, Stéphane, ill. II. Title. • PZ7.Q41553Gra 2007 • [E]—dc22
The art was rendered in pencil, watercolor, and gouache on Strathmore 3-ply bristol 500.

I tried not to fall asleep,
staying overnight at Grandmama
and Granddad's cottage on the lake.

I had it all figured out—listening to owls, counting stars, playing shadow games, way past my bedtime.
I wasn't going to miss anything.

Staying awake is how I knew when Granddad scuffed
down the hallway, while the sky was still blue-black and
the stars shone like night-lights.
"Why are you up, in the night?" I asked him.
"I could ask you the same thing," he said.

I followed him to the kitchen and watched as he made breakfast and put his vest on.

"Where you going?" I asked.

"Meeting my fishing buddy," he said.

"Oooooh . . . fishing . . . Can I come too?"

Granddad started to shake his head, then stopped long enough to take a good look at me.

I stood just as tall as I could, so I would look every bit as old as I was.

"Can you keep real quiet so the fish don't know we're there?" he asked.

"You bet," I said.

"Can you row the boat without making it turn in circles?"

"With my eyes closed," I told him.

He raised one eyebrow and I quickly added, "But I promise to keep them open."

"Can you put a worm on a hook?"

I hesitated a minute, not so sure about that one, but I took a deep breath and said, "No problem."

Granddad seemed to add it all up in his head.

He put on his favorite fishing hat, then left a note for Grandmama.

Gone fishing.
See you for lunch.
Love,
Ed and Sara

"Yippee!" I hooted, then remembered the part about being quiet and whispered, "Yippee."

We pushed off the dock with a splash,
sending ripples across the glassy lake.
Steam lifted from the water like clouds.

Way out on the lake it was quiet, except for the smooth sound of fishing line sailing through the air and landing with a *plop* in the water.

"Watch close," Granddad said. "That's how I learned."

I had almost forgotten about Granddad's fishing buddy, and it seemed he had too.

I asked, "Why did we leave without your buddy?"

"He'll meet us out here," Granddad said.

We were the first boat on the lake, but just as the ducks and geese flew in, one by one, boats began to roost on the rippled water.

Granddad knew everyone. He smiled and waved. Sometimes they traded fishing secrets, sometimes a joke.

He pointed to me and said, "This is my granddaughter, Sara.
She's a keeper."

"Was that your fishing buddy?" I asked after each person passed by.
"Nope," he said time after time.
Then we always got quiet again, so the fish would come.

Granddad reached into a bucket of dirt and
pulled out a worm that coiled around as it swayed
from his fingertips. In his other hand he carefully
held a hook.
I looked at the hook,
then the worm,
then back again.

I needed a plan.

I remembered the licorice that Grandmama had filled my pockets with yesterday. I pulled out a little bit and slid it onto the hook.

I smiled nervously at Granddad, expecting him to stop me.

He didn't.

And I was glad.

We waited a long time. Our fishing lines
hung in the water like the tails of fallen kites.
Suddenly a shadow skimmed over the lake.

A heron glided over our heads and landed near the lily pads. He stood statue-still, watching the water. In a blink, he plucked a fish right out.

Granddad smiled. He said, "Row."

"Which way?" I asked.

"Over there," he said, pointing to where the heron balanced on one skinny leg. The heron eyed us both, quickly, then gazed into the water. He waded, stirring up more fish.

We cast our lines near the heron. My bobber went under. I held tight to my pole, and wound the reel just like Granddad.

"I caught one!" I hollered.

"It's a beauty!" cheered Granddad.

He was real proud, I could tell. But he wanted to catch one too.

"You'll get one," I told him.

I put a piece of licorice on his hook.

After a while the heron flew away. I squeezed my eyes nearly shut, trying to follow his flight into the bright sky. He swooped and landed near the opposite shore.

"Row," said Granddad.

This time I knew exactly where. We followed the heron. Right then I figured out who Granddad's fishing buddy was, the best fisherman on the lake.

We caught lots of fish that day,
Granddad,
the heron,
and I.

While we tied the boat to the pier, I asked Granddad, "When are you going out with your fishing buddy again?"

He winked, put his big fishing hat on my head, and said, "When are you coming back to the lake?"